RED HANDED

Titles in Dark Reads:

Blood Moon
Barbara Catchpole

Doctor Jekyll and Little Miss Hyde
Tony Lee

Red Handed
Ann Evans

Ringtone
Tommy Donbavand

Ship of the Dead
Alex Woolf

Straw Men
Ann Evans

The Black-Eyed Girl
Tim Collins

The Girl in the Wall
Tommy Donbavand

Badger Publishing Limited, Oldmedow Road, Hardwick Industrial Estate, King's Lynn PE30 4JJ
Telephone: 01438 791037

www.badgerlearning.co.uk

RED HANDED

ANN EVANS

Badger
LEARNING

Red Handed ISBN 978-1-78464-095-8

Publisher: Susan Ross
Senior Editor: Danny Pearson
Publishing Assistant: Claire Morgan
Copyeditor: Cheryl Lanyon
Designer: Bigtop Design Ltd
Illustrator: Amit Tayal

2 4 6 8 10 9 7 5 3 1

CHAPTER 1
THIEF

Nick Moss was good at nicking things. Sweets, fags, cash. Today he nicked the biggest thing ever.

An oil painting.

The man in the painting looked like him – handsome, smart.

Nick hung it over a damp patch. It gave his bedsit an air of elegance.

Nicking it had been easy. Now he felt like going on a nicking spree again.

Yeah, right now!

Excitement rose inside him.

He grabbed some tools – a hammer and crowbar.

"Wish me luck," he said, grinning at the man in the painting.

The man in the painting seemed to grin back.

It was his mind playing tricks. Nick knew that. Still, it made him feel good.

No one argues with a man with a crowbar!

Nick went home happy, with wads
of money.

Much later, as he went to bed, he felt it...
A warm breath on the back of his neck.

"Who's there?"

Silence.

Just the ticking of the clock.

CHAPTER 2
THE VOICE

An icy shiver ran down Nick's spine. Someone was here, in the room.

His skin crawled.

He ran to the door.

"STAY!"

The word rang out, filling the room, filling his head. A dark, evil voice.

Terror froze him to the spot.

"KILL FOR ME!"

Nick wanted to run… screaming.

"Who… who are you?"

"I AM DORIAN GRAY… GO KILL FOR ME!"

Nick wanted to say NO! He was a thief.
Not a murderer.

But he turned and walked out of his bedsit
as if in a dream.

Something walked with him, into the night.
A dark, evil thing.

It was easy to kill.

Nick felt like he was a puppet.
With someone pulling the strings.

CHAPTER 3
GONE!

When the terrible deed was done, Nick staggered home.

His hands felt sticky with blood. Yet they were clean.

When he looked in the mirror, he looked just the same. Handsome. Smart.

But when he looked at the painting...

CHAPTER 4
KILLING SPREE

Next morning, Nick hoped it had all been a bad dream.

But the man in the painting was still smiling – an ugly, murderer's smile.

And his hands still dripped with blood.

In a rage Nick tried to rip it from the wall.

"NO!"

Nick fell back.

"BRING ME GOLD AND DIAMONDS!"

Nick's eyes lit up. Nicking stuff. Yeah,
he could do that.

He could do anything!

Nicking jewellery was easy. And so what if
they tried to put up a fight?

So it went on. Day after day. Night after night. Nick stole and killed.

And got away with it.

"You take care of me, don't you?" he said to the painting. "You get uglier and uglier. **My** guilt is written all over **your** face!"

CHAPTER 5
GUILTY!

One morning, the painting looked so terrible, Nick felt sick.

It had to go.

It took all his strength to drag it from the wall.

It screamed and raged.

At last he got it outside and into a skip.

The police were waiting.

"Nick Moss, we're arresting you for murder and theft..."

"No way! I'm innocent."

"Got you red-handed, mate!" said the policeman.

It was true. Nick's hands dripped blood. Guilt was written all over his face.

"No!" he cried.

He looked back at the painting. It was perfect again.

STORY FACTS

The idea for this story was inspired by a famous novel by Oscar Wilde called *The Picture of Dorian Gray*. It was published in 1891.

Oscar Wilde (1854–1900) was an Irish playwright and poet.

The Picture of Dorian Gray was the only novel Oscar Wilde wrote.

The novel is based around the same idea. Someone does not get away with his crimes, even when he thinks he has.

The author of this book, Ann Evans, wrote that Nick put the painting in a skip. That way, someone else might find it. The terrible power of the painting could carry on – until someone is strong enough to resist it.

QUESTIONS

What had Nick Moss stolen today?
(page 5)

What did Nick feel that night as he went
to bed?
(page 10)

What did the dark, evil voice shout?
(page 12)

How did Nick feel as he walked out of
the room?
(page 16)

What did Dorian Gray want Nick to
get him?
(page 22)

Where did the author get her idea for
the story from?
(page 30)

Ann Evans began writing as a hobby over 30 years ago. That hobby turned into a career and a way of life. She loves writing for all ages, including adults. She also writes non-fiction for many different magazines and says writing is the best job ever!

Amit Tayal was born and educated in India. From 5th Grade he used to trade superhero sketches for help with his homework. He started his career as an animator in Delhi and is now based in Reading, UK. Amit likes to travel and loves console gaming.